For my six precious lambs; even though you are big now,
you will always be my little ones. And for Lizzy—my first grandlamby
—with love, L.E.

For Faith —D.M.

·

For information address Disney · Hyperion Books, 114 Fifth Avenue, New York, New York 10011-5690

First Edition

10 9 8 7 6 5 4 3 2 1

ILS No. F850-6835-5

274   2009

Printed in Singapore · Reinforced binding

Library of Congress Cataloging-in-Publication Data

Evans, Lezlie. · Who loves the little lamb? / written by Lezlie Evans ; illustrated by David McPhail.— 1st ed.

p. cm. · Summary: Rhyming text reveals that, although baby animals are not always perfect,
their mothers love them and help them through difficult moments.

ISBN-13: 978-1-4231-1659-2 · ISBN-10: 1-4231-1659-3

[1. Stories in rhyme. 2. Mother and child—Fiction. 3. Animals—Infancy—Fiction.]

I. McPhail, David, 1940- ill. II. Title.

PZ8.3.E915Who 2010   [E]—dc22   2009015896

Visit www.hyperionbooksforchildren.com

Who Loves the Little Lamb?

by Lezlie Evans ❋ illustrated by David McPhail

DISNEP · HYPERION BOOKS / NEW YORK

Who loves the fussy lamb?

"No more crying, here I am." Mama loves her little lamb.

Who loves the messy pup?

"Come on, dear, I'll help clean up." Mama loves her little pup.

Who loves the pouting calf?

"I'll tickle you and make you laugh." Mama loves her little calf.

Who loves the noisy bird?

"Sing sweetly, please, you'll still be heard." Mama loves her little bird.

Who loves the bumbling boar?

"That's all right, there's plenty more." Mama loves her little boar.

Who loves the naughty kid?

"We can fix that broken lid." Mama loves her little kid.

Who loves the prickly porcupine?

"Don't worry, hon, you look divine!" Mama loves her porcupine.

Who loves the hungry 'beest?

"Here's your favorite—what a feast!" Mama loves her wildebeest.

Who loves the dirty cub?

"Time to wash, I'll help you scrub." Mama loves her little cub.

Who loves the sleepy 'roo?

"Climb on in, I'll carry you." Mama loves her kangaroo.

"Tell me, Mama, is it true—
do you care the whole day through?
Even when I do things wrong,
do you love me all day long?"

"Yes, my precious child, it's true—no matter what you say or do.
From dawn till after day is done, Mama loves her little one."